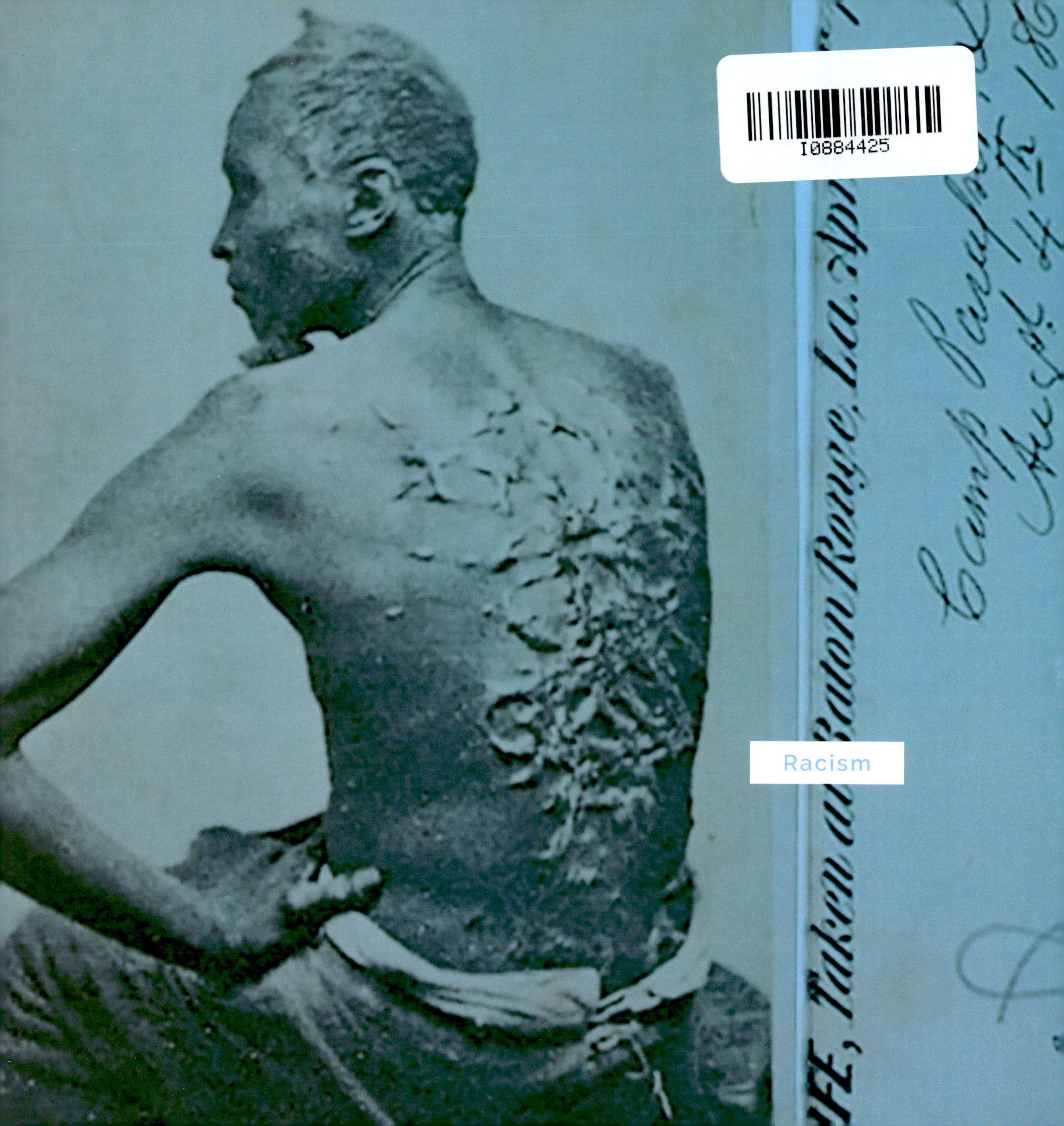

Racism

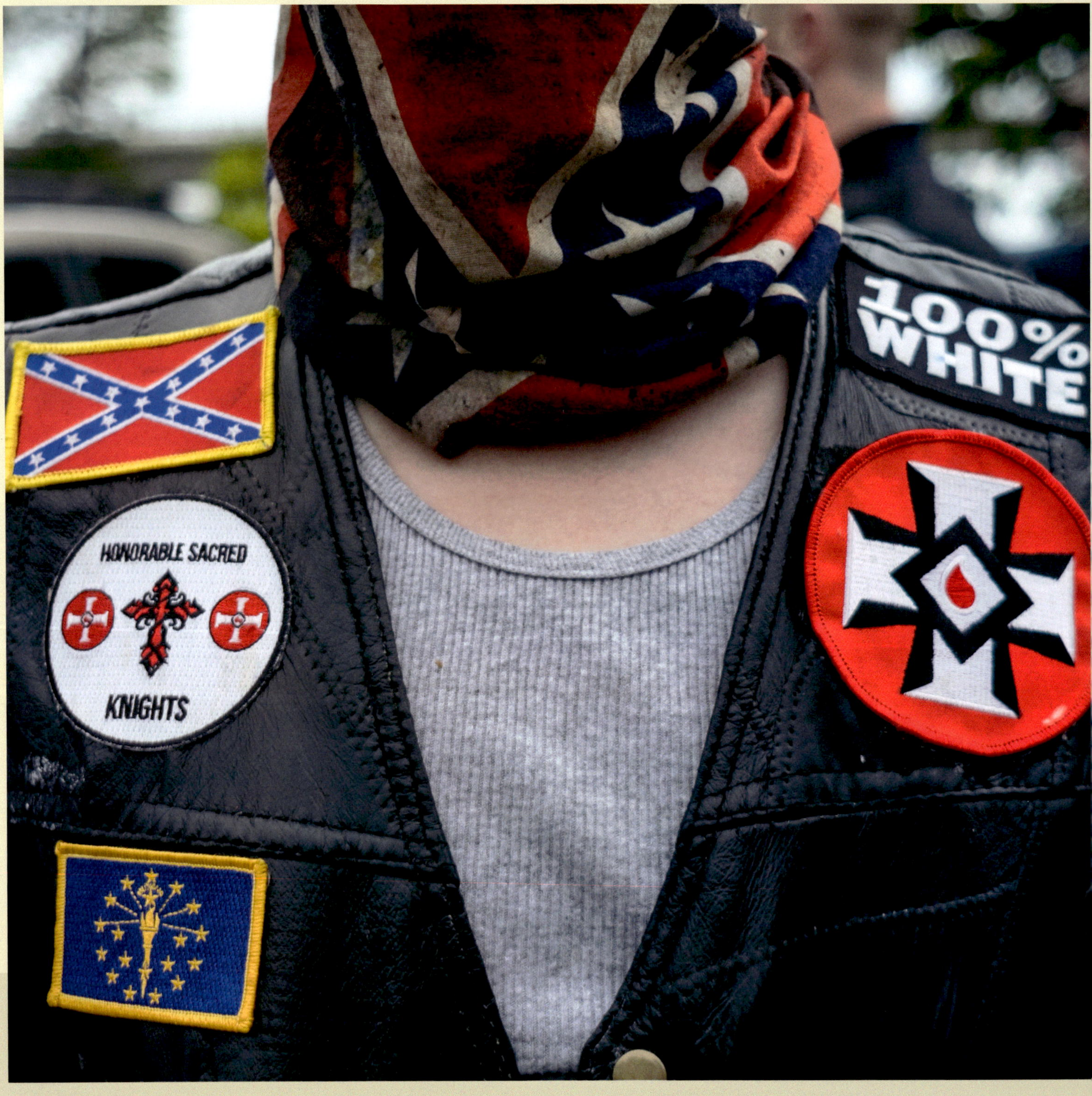
100% WHITE
HONORABLE SACRED
KNIGHTS

Racism

Mari Bolte

Living in AMERICA

CREATIVE EDUCATION

CREATIVE PAPERBACKS

Published by Creative Education and Creative Paperbacks
P.O. Box 227, Mankato, Minnesota 56002
Creative Education and Creative Paperbacks are imprints
of The Creative Company
www.thecreativecompany.us

Book design by Graham Morgan (www.bluedes.com)
Art direction by Tom Morgan
Edited by Jill Kalz

Images by Getty (Bettmann, Carol Lee Rose, drakuliren, Hulton Archive, Megan Jelinger /Anadolu Agency, mikroman6, MPI, Nastasic, Pictures from History, Spencer Platt, Ted Soqui, Visions of America), Unsplash (Andy MacMillan, Clay Banks, mana5280), Wikimedia Commons (Cowan's Auctions, Dick DeMarsico, Emw, George M. Weister)

Library of Congress Cataloging-in-Publication Data
Names: Bolte, Mari, author.
Title: Racism / by Mari Bolte.
Description: Mankato, Minnesota : Creative Education and Creative Paperbacks, [2025] | Series: Living in America | Includes bibliographical references and index. | Audience: Ages 12–15 | Audience: Grades 7–9 | Summary: "A social studies title for young adults that examines the history, power, and effects of discrimination, prejudice, and racism in the United States of America. Includes sidebars, real-person profiles, a glossary, a timeline, and further resources"—Provided by publisher.
Identifiers: LCCN 2023047140 (print) | LCCN 2023047141 (ebook) | ISBN 9781640269118 (library binding) | ISBN 9781682774618 (paperback) | ISBN 9798889890799 (ebook)
Subjects: LCSH: Racism—United States—History—Juvenile literature. | Race discrimination—United States—History—Juvenile literature. | United States—Race relations—History—Juvenile literature. Classification: LCC E184.A1 B5956 2025 (print) | LCC E184.A1 (ebook) | DDC 305.800973—dc23/eng/20231120
LC record available at https://lccn.loc.gov/2023047140
LC ebook record available at https://lccn.loc.gov/2023047141

Printed in China

Civil rights leader Martin Luther King, Jr. addresses supporters in Washington, D.C., in 1963.

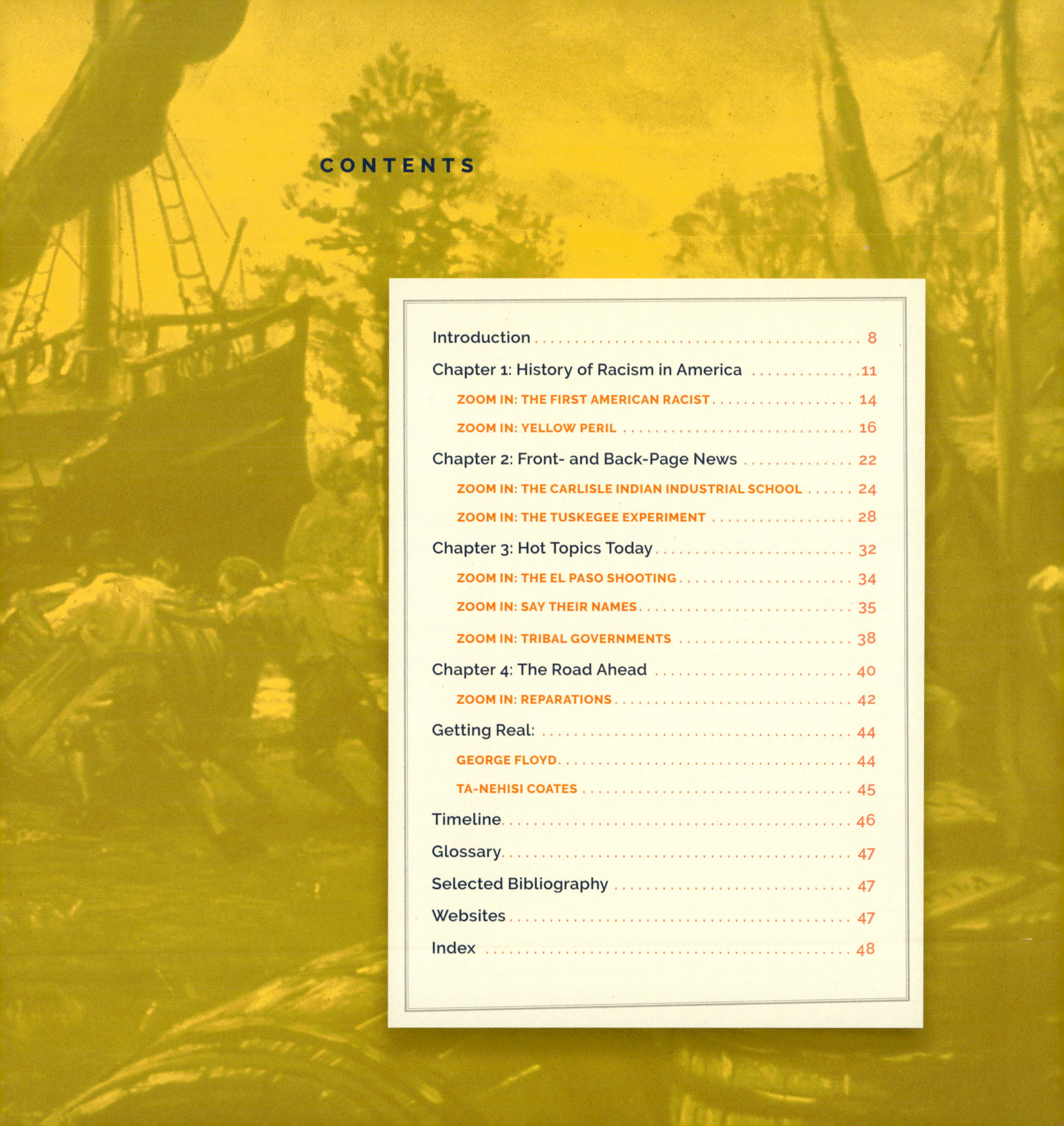

CONTENTS

Introduction

Few subjects are as divisive in American society today as racism. Stories about racial profiling, police brutality, and discrimination go viral every day. People take to the streets to protest, experts give interviews on the news, and politicians declare they will make change. But racism goes deeper than headlines and video clips. For some, it's part of their everyday lives and experiences.

Racism is discrimination or prejudice against a person based on their race or ethnicity. There are four major types: personal/internalized, interpersonal, institutional, and structural. Each plays a role in giving one group of people an advantage over others.

- **Personal racism** shapes our private thoughts. The ideas that flash through our brains when we see or think about a different group of people are learned. They affect how we respond to and interact with that group.
- **Interpersonal racism** occurs between two people verbally or physically. Bullying, harassment, and violence are examples.
- **Institutional racism** can be seen in discriminatory policies and practices applied to different groups of people. It continues inequalities in areas such as civil rights, education, and income by reinforcing perceived differences between groups.
- **Structural racism** is built into our laws and rules, creating advantages for the majority group and oppressing or harming the other groups. This type of racism prevents people from getting proper health care, education, jobs, housing, or legal help.

Understanding the history, power, and effects of racism in the United States is how life can be improved for everyone—but especially for minority groups who have lived through it.

Civil rights protesters in Tennessee, 1968

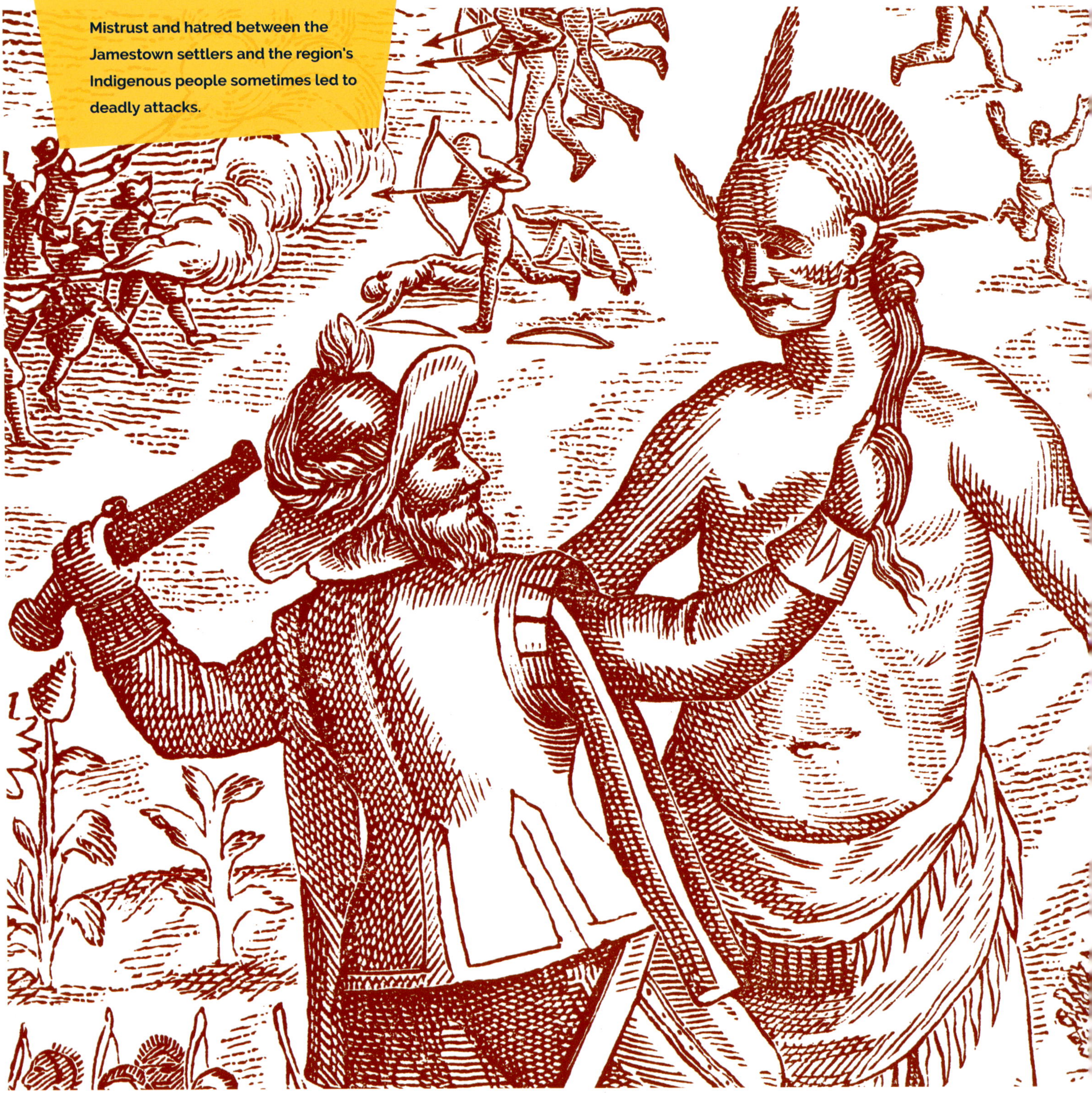

Mistrust and hatred between the Jamestown settlers and the region's Indigenous people sometimes led to deadly attacks.

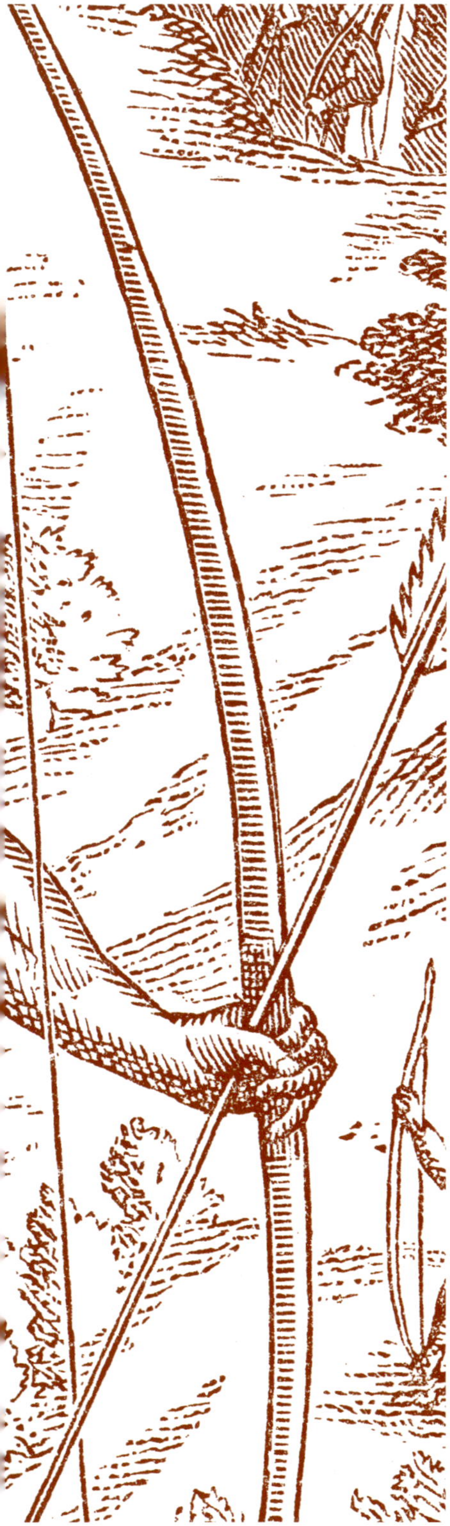

CHAPTER 1:

History of Racism in America

The first people arrived in North America as early as 30,000 years ago. They came on boats from eastern Eurasia, following the rich resources along the western coast of North America.

Later, around 13,000 to 13,500 years ago, a land bridge opened. It connected Siberia to Alaska and Canada. Another group of people, called the Clovis, used this bridge and spread across the land. They moved to eastern North America and south toward Mexico. **Indigenous** people today are ancestors of the Clovis settlers. European settlers arrived hundreds of years later. By then, about 60 million American Indians, grouped into roughly 600 different tribal nations, were living in North America.

In 1607, the first permanent **colony** was founded in Jamestown, Virginia. The colonizers struggled that first year. They faced starvation and disease. They also experienced conflict with the

Indigenous people. Spanish explorers had already tried to claim land and resources for their own. One of the first Jamestown ships was attacked before it even landed. But eventually, the native people decided to welcome the new visitors.

Powhatan was an Indigenous leader in the Chesapeake Bay area. He shared food and knowledge on how to grow crops with the colonists. But rather than grow their own food, the colonists relied on the tribes to keep them fed. Because the Indigenous people weren't white and Christian, many colonists did not consider them equals. They were seen as lesser beings. Captain John Smith used force and threats to get what he wanted for the colony.

In 1619, a General Assembly was formed. This early government was made up of white male landowners. That same year, the English ship *White Lion*, carrying about 20 enslaved people from Africa, arrived in the colony. The ship's captain traded the human cargo for food. Some people consider this to be the first account of enslaved people in the New World.

Until the 17th century, white convicts and indentured servants had done much of the work in the colonies. But servants were owed land, weapons, and supplies once their terms were up. This labor system ate into profits and threatened rich landowners. Landowners saw that Africans knew how to grow food and raise animals that did well in the colonies. Enslaving them would ensure a steady labor supply while denying them the same rights as white workers. Racial slavery seemed like the answer.

People from Africa were imported and sold to America for nearly 200 years. Then, in 1808, Congress stopped the slave trade between countries. Slave traders didn't like competing with European ships. Many others saw the Transatlantic slave trade as inhumane. However, it didn't stop many of those same people from owning slaves themselves. Once buying and selling between countries ended, they felt that their main work had been accomplished. **Abolitionism** wouldn't have a strong voice again for another 20 to 30 years.

Into the mid-1800s, enslaved Black men were valuable commodities—objects easily bought and sold.

ZOOM IN: THE FIRST AMERICAN RACIST

Author Ibram X. Kendi, founder of the Center for Antiracist Research at Boston University, recently identified politician John Pory as America's first known racist. In 1600, Pory published a translation of *A Geographical Historie of Africa*. This work was full of racist stereotypes about African people. In his introduction, Pory theorized that Black people had been cursed. In 1619, Pory was elected the first Speaker of the Virginia Assembly. In that role, he recognized the need for tobacco as a crop—and the need for more workers to grow it. The *White Lion*, with its cargo of enslaved people from Africa, sailed into Virginia at just the right time.

Slave owners had to think of a new way to get fresh workers. Slave auctions began taking place in towns and cities around the country. Around 1.2 million enslaved men, women, and children were bought and sold between 1760 and 1860.

Black people were not the only people who lost their homes and families simply because of their race. The Europeans had brought more to America than goods and religion. They also brought diseases against which the Indigenous people had no defense. Across North, Central, and South America, colonizers caused the deaths of about 56 million Indigenous people over 100 years. Sometimes, it was accidental. Other times, it was intentional. For example, handing out supplies contaminated with smallpox was one way to spread the disease. By 1809, a smallpox vaccine had been created. However, it wasn't offered to Indigenous people until the Indian Vaccination Act of 1832. By this time, many tribes had been decimated.

As more white people arrived from other continents, they needed room to spread out. Politicians argued that the Indigenous people did not need all the space they had lived on for thousands of years. And, they continued, were they people at all? Their culture was not European. They did not own land. They were not godly. And they did not farm the land like white farmers to get the most out of it. Eradicating Indigenous people was a natural step. In fact, the U.S. government encouraged it. It offered rewards for native peoples' skulls and scalps. The military burned homes and crops. They killed anyone who stood in their way.

In 1830, the U.S. Congress passed the Indian Removal Act. The Cherokee, Creek, Seminole, Chickasaw, and Creek people were forced to travel 2,200 miles (3,541 kilometers) from their traditional lands to an area in Oklahoma. The Trail of Tears led to the deaths of thousands of people. Starvation, disease, and overcrowding met the survivors at the end of the trail.

In 1845, a belief called Manifest Destiny became popular. It said that God wanted white people to spread democracy and capitalism across

The "unlimited" supply of enslaved people in the 1700s and 1800s was perfect for growing tobacco and other labor-intensive crops.

the land. White populations spread, and Indigenous ones dwindled. As waves of settlers moved west, they discovered untapped resources. The land was untouched. The waters were full of fish. There was gold to mine and railroads to build. Workers were needed. So, between the 1840s and 1850s, young men from China were brought over as laborers. The pay was low, and the work was dangerous. Hundreds of workers lost their lives. But for many, it was a welcome chance to earn money.

One of the root causes of the Civil War (1861–65) was slavery. The Southern states wanted to continue enslaving people and expand the territories where it was legal. It was their way of life and their source of income. The Northern states were opposed to this idea. The founding of the United States was based on the idea that everyone was equal. Slavery went against this idea. Enslaved people could not vote, but their work—their unpaid work—contributed to the country's success. When the two sides couldn't agree, a war ensued.

Following the war, Black people began searching for the family they had lost. But it was hard, sometimes impossible, without birth or marriage certificates, written records, or last names—all things enslaved people had systematically been denied. Even if legal documents existed, Black people did not have the right to see them, nor could many read. Teaching enslaved people how to read and write had been forbidden. It was a way for the majority white population to prevent resistance. Even Thomas Jefferson, who spoke out for liberty and equality, did not teach his slaves to read. He was afraid literate people would demand their freedom.

Losing a large amount of free labor meant finding workers from other places. By 1870, 20 percent of California's workforce was Chinese. Then, the economy crashed. A depression in 1876 made jobs hard to find. Unemployed white workers declared that

ZOOM IN: YELLOW PERIL

Yellow Peril is the Western fear that Asian people will invade and take over the United States with their beliefs and ways of life. White supremacists have an additional fear that Asian people will marry white partners and have biracial children. Dating back to the mid-1800s, Asian clothing, physical traits, and culture were portrayed as cartoonish, undesirable, or even evil. In peace time, traits associated with the Asian "model minority" myth—hardworking, studious, passive—were seen as desirable. However, in war time, these traits were framed as job competition, pitting Asian and white workers against each other.

Racist publications in the late 1800s accused Chinese immigrants of stealing jobs from white workers.

the Chinese were taking their jobs. The Chinese **Exclusion** Act was passed in 1882. For 10 years, Chinese **immigrants** were not allowed to come to America. The act was extended again after the 10 years were up. By 1890, if 2 percent of a nationality already lived in America, no one else from that country could enter.

The Chinese Exclusion Act was passed, but hard, dirty jobs still needed to be done. Railroad companies began to hire people from Mexico. By the early 1900s, as many as 60 percent of their workers were Mexican. Immigration limits were passed in 1921 and 1924, but Mexico was excluded. Border stations were set up to let Mexican workers cross to live and work. Around 600,000 Mexican immigrants lived formally in the United States by 1930.

The Great Depression began in 1929 and lasted for 10 years. Social security programs were started to help keep people out of poverty. However, agricultural and domestic workers were not included. Many of these workers were from minority populations.

White workers fled cities and moved to California looking for work. Once again, they saw nonwhite workers as direct competition. Removing "undocumented aliens" would free up jobs for white Americans. More than 400,000 Mexican Americans were forcibly removed from their homes and deported to Mexico by the federal government. Many others fled before it could happen.

President Franklin Roosevelt repealed the Chinese Exclusion Act in 1943. The first naturalized Chinese American citizen was Edward Bing Kan. Naturalization is how citizenship is granted to a lawful permanent resident who meets certain criteria. Filipino and Indian immigrants could gain citizenship shortly after.

However, World War II (1939–45) proved that being a citizen was not a guaranteed protection, especially if a person was part of a minority group. On December 7, 1941, Japan bombed Pearl Harbor in Hawaii. In February 1942, President Roosevelt signed **Executive Order** 9066. This forced 120,000 Japanese Americans—citizens or not—to **internment** camps. Some German and Italian nationals were detained in camps as well.

The Emancipation Proclamation had been issued by President Abraham Lincoln in 1863, during the Civil War. While it didn't end slavery, it was an important step forward. However, in 1877, a a system of racially motivated laws called Jim Crow laws were enacted in southern U.S. states. These were laws that treated Black people as second-class citizens, keeping them apart from white society. The dominant view was that white people were superior. Whites were the majority population, and they held positions of political and economic power. They could control the country's narrative.

The U.S. civil rights movement rose to prominence in the 1950s and 1960s. It was a nationwide nonviolent movement that began to abolish racial **segregation**. People participated in boycotts, sit-ins, and marches to fight for Black equality. It

About two-thirds of the people interned in the Manzanar camp, in a desert area of California, were U.S. citizens by birth.

was dangerous and sometimes deadly work. Black leaders and their families were threatened, and their homes were bombed. They were beaten and shot. Hate groups such as the Ku Klux Klan, which had been around since 1867, began to rise again. Activists were murdered, and their killers were never brought to justice.

But the fight led to progress. The Civil Rights Act of 1964 and the Voting Rights Act of 1965 were passed. Eventually, Jim Crow laws were abolished. Public education was desegregated. The door was finally opening for people of color.

Today, quotes from civil rights leaders such as Martin Luther King, Jr. are widely shared. But at the time, most white Americans disagreed with those words. King was one of the most hated men in America. His views on racial equality, the Vietnam War, and workers' rights were highly unpopular. The week he was assassinated, nearly 75 percent of Americans disapproved of what he stood for.

Fixing deep-seated systematic racism and practices doesn't happen overnight. For years to come, minorities still made less money in the workforce. Contracts and loans were still given to white-owned businesses more often than to those of nonwhites. As recently as 2021, nearly 20 percent of all Black people in the United States lived below the poverty line. It was the lowest it had been since the poverty line was first measured in 1959, but the number was still the highest of all races. Hispanic populations were nearly at 16 percent. Around 7 percent of white populations lived in poverty—a number that hasn't changed much over the years.

Martin Luther King, Jr. fought for racial equality through peaceful protests such as marches and sit-ins.

CHAPTER 2:

Front- and Back-Page News

The 14th **Amendment** was ratified on July 9, 1868, after slavery was abolished. It was meant to help newly freed Black people by granting citizenship to anyone "born or naturalized in the United States."

In 1898, the Supreme Court ruled on *U.S. v Wong Ark*. At the time, the Chinese Exclusion Act denied citizenship to Chinese immigrants. They could also not become naturalized citizens. Wong Kim Ark was born in California. His parents, both Chinese citizens, lived there. When Wong was 21 years old, he and his family went to China to visit family. When they tried to go home, Wong was told he could not re-enter the United States because he was not a citizen. The Supreme Court decided that Wong was an automatic citizen according to the 14th Amendment because he was born in the United States.

President Donald Trump said repeatedly while in office (2016–21) that he intended to do away with the 14th Amendment. Some conservative legal scholars argued that the United States has

The Statue of Liberty, dedicated in 1886, is a U.S. symbol of freedom and hope.

changed a lot since the 14th Amendment was passed. Slavery, for example, no longer exists. These scholars believed that the amendment was not meant to apply to children born to noncitizens. Trump agreed and believed he could issue an Executive Order, ending the amendment. He was unsuccessful in his attempt.

The Supreme Court has seen many cases regarding the 14th Amendment since its ratification. Workers' rights, a citizen's right to privacy, and segregation have all been the subject of cases. So has interracial marriage.

Before 1967, interracial marriage in the United States was illegal. It had been banned since Maryland's first law banning it in 1691. The idea was to keep the white race pure and avoid upsetting the racial order as seen by white society. The white majority believed mixed-race children would blur the line between slave and master. An example of structural racism, the interracial marriage ban was a way to elevate white people over everyone else. Allowing unions between races would imply equality existed.

Virginia's General Assembly's act aimed to prevent "Negroes, mulattoes, and Indians intermarrying with English, or other white women." Anyone found breaking this law would be forced to leave the state. In 1848, the government went even further. Jail sentences were given, and anyone involved in an interracial marriage could be harshly fined or even tarred and feathered. The next year, the state declared that all marriages between Black and white

ZOOM IN: THE CARLISLE INDIAN INDUSTRIAL SCHOOL

The Carlisle Indian Industrial School operated from 1879 to 1918. It was founded by the U.S. government. Thousands of Indigenous children—as well as adult men—were abducted by federal agents and sent to the school in Pennsylvania. They represented more than 100 different communities. They did not speak the same language or have the same way of life. The Carlisle Indian Industrial School's goal was to "kill the Indian to save the Man." The students were taught how to live in white society, abandoning their heritage. Their hair was cut. Their names were changed. Anyone caught speaking languages other than English was abused.

"Reformed" student athletes of the Carlisle Indian Industrial School

people were "absolutely void." Over the next 100 years, interracial marriage became illegal in 24 U.S. states.

In 1958, Mildred Jeter married Richard Loving. Jeter was Black and Indigenous. Loving was white. Their wedding was held in the District of Columbia, where the marriage was legal. The couple moved to Bowling Green, Virginia, soon after, unaware that the state had laws banning interracial marriage. Five weeks after their wedding, the couple was arrested in the middle of the night. They were given a choice—spend a year in jail or leave the state for 25 years.

The family moved to Washington, D.C., but they missed their family in Virginia. Their case was heard by the U.S. Supreme Court. Their lawyer stated that the law went against the 14th Amendment. "These are not health and welfare laws," he said. "These are slavery laws, pure and simple." On June 12, 1967, the Supreme Court justices agreed, stating that the interracial marriage law did, in fact, violate the 14th Amendment.

On September 11, 2001, the terrorist group Al-Qaeda carried out a deadly attack against the United States. Two airplanes were hijacked and flown into the World Trade Center in New York City. Another airplane targeted the Pentagon, just outside Washington, D.C. A fourth crashed into a field in Pennsylvania. In total, nearly 3,000 people were killed.

The 9/11 attack changed the world. Al-Qaeda had not targeted a specific race or ethnic group. But their hijackers had been from Middle Eastern countries. Muslim Americans quickly found themselves at the center of racist attacks at home. The false idea that many of them knew about the 9/11 attack in advance spread distrust across the country. Then, the United States began a 20-year military mission to Afghanistan to remove the terrorists who had carried out the attack. Hate crimes against Muslim people in the United States skyrocketed. Having a Muslim-sounding name or wearing a head covering in public often resulted in a verbal or physical attack.

9/11 terrorists flew the first airplane into the north tower and the second into the south tower 17 minutes later.

After 9/11, the National Security Agency (NSA) began watching people under the Foreign Intelligence Surveillance Act, Section 702. The program secretly tracked phone calls and emails of millions of Americans without their knowledge. The NSA claimed they were targeting people living overseas, but they also monitored U.S.

ZOOM IN: THE TUSKEGEE EXPERIMENT

In 1932, the U.S. Public Health Service paired with the Tuskegee Institute to study a disease called syphilis. Six hundred Black men were studied. They were mostly poor farmers who had never been to a doctor before. They were not given details about the study, nor were they asked for consent. Doctors observed the men and gave them placebos, even though a cure was available starting in 1947. Some men went blind. Some lost their minds. Others unwittingly passed on the disease to their wives and children. The Tuskegee experiment went on until 1972, when someone shared what was happening with the media.

citizens who had family in other countries. Often, these citizens were part of the Muslim community.

The American Civil Liberties Union (ACLU) brought the NSA to trial in 2006. The trial court agreed with the ACLU, saying the program violated the rights of U.S. citizens. However, the U.S. Court of Appeals overturned it a year later. They said that the ACLU could not prove they were the ones being surveilled. The Supreme Court refused to hear the case at all. And the unconstitutional information gathering didn't end there. As late as 2023, the Federal Bureau of Investigation (FBI) was using the Act to gather information. They tracked protesters, racial justice coordinators, political party donors, and activists.

Some racist acts make the front-page news and go all the way to the Supreme Court. Other times, racism happens quietly, as a part of daily life. Nearly 19 percent of the total U.S. population today is Hispanic, with ties to Mexico, Cuba, Puerto Rico, and other Spanish-speaking countries. Despite that strong number, structural and institutional racism in housing, education, and the job market continue to work against them daily. Prejudice continues against people

Border fences between Mexico and the United States affect families in both countries.

Generations of systemic racism continue to disproportionately affect American Indian women and children today.

with Hispanic last names, people who speak Spanish, and people who were born outside the United States. Immigrants from Central and South America have been compared to gang members, criminals, and rapists. Political **rhetoric** conjures up images of violent Latinx people invading from the south. "Crisis" and "invasion" are words often associated with the Mexican American border, used to drive fear and insecurity in the white community.

In 2018, a study found that two-thirds of Americans do not believe that Indigenous people experience discrimination. Yet, American Indians are the nonwhite group most likely to be killed by police. Nearly all Indigenous women have experienced violence by someone outside their community. Young people are the most likely to take their own lives, and graduation rates are at the bottom of any racial group. They are also twice as likely to be sent to prison for minor crimes.

Compared with other racial groups, American Indians are given little representation in the media. Their history is rarely taught in schools. Discrimination against them usually receives scant coverage by the mainstream news. Most of what students outside American Indian communities are taught about Indigenous people talks about them in the past tense. Internet image searches bring up mostly historical photographs. Today, there are 573 federally recognized tribal nations living across the United States. That's more than five million people. Ignoring the tribes' individuality, histories, and contributions to society is a deep form of racism.

CHAPTER 3:

Hot Topics Today

In the early 1700s, a common fear held by many white plantation owners was that the enslaved people working their land would revolt. Owners needed a way to police these people and to chase down anyone who escaped. Enslaved people were costly property.

Slave patrols, made up largely of white men, were formed to find, capture, and return those who had run away. Escaped slaves were harshly punished. After the Emancipation Proclamation, the slave patrols turned into militia-style groups. Their mission was to control Black people and make the white majority feel safe. They implemented segregation and used fear and violence to stop anyone who tried to cross the line. Then, the 14th Amendment was passed. The groups began enforcing racist Jim Crow laws that continued to keep white and Black people apart. The laws affected nearly every part of a Black person's daily life. They separated Black and white people at schools, parks, movie

The secretive hate group known as the Ku Klux Klan gained traction in the 1860s as slave patrols faded.

ZOOM IN: THE EL PASO SHOOTING

In 2019, a gunman opened fire at a Walmart in El Paso, Texas. He chose the store because it was near the Mexican American border. He killed 22 people that day and injured another 23. The shooter, a white man from Dallas, had written a four-page manifesto justifying his attack as a "response to the Hispanic invasion of Texas." Racist rhetoric used by politicians, including President Donald Trump, was included in the manifesto as well. In February 2023, the killer pled guilty to hate crimes and was sentenced to 90 consecutive life terms in prison.

theaters, restrooms, and on public transportation. Militia groups patrolled Black communities to show a constant presence. They were there to remind Black citizens that they were being watched. Groups had ranks, uniforms, and a code of command. These ideas moved north as cities needed a way to control growing immigrant populations. Boston, Massachusetts, was the first city to create an official police department in 1838.

Police brutality in the United States has been a hot topic as long as there has been a police force. In 1929, a study in Chicago found that Black people made up 30 percent of victims killed by the police, even though they made up only 5 percent of the total population. Those numbers did not change much over the next 100 years. In 2022, Black people made up 13 percent of the total population but 27 percent of fatal shootings by police officers.

How the history of America is told depends on who is telling the story. For many years, U.S. schoolchildren were taught the nation's history from the white perspective only: The first colonists and the Indigenous people worked together to help each other thrive; the Founding Fathers believed that "all men are created equal"; settlers moved onto empty land, and any American Indians they

ZOOM IN: SAY THEIR NAMES

Black people are up to three times more likely than white people to be killed by a police officer. Some receive media attention. Many others do not. In 2014, **Eric Garner** was accused of illegally selling cigarettes. A police officer choked him. Garner said, "I can't breathe!" 11 times before he lost consciousness and died. **Philando Castile** was driving home in 2017 when a police officer pulled him over. As he reached for his driver's license, the officer shot and killed him. Castile's girlfriend and young daughter were also in the car. In 2020, police believed the apartment of **Breonna Taylor** in Louisville, Kentucky, was involved in a drug deal. In the middle of the night, they forced their way in. Breonna was shot at least eight times and died shortly after.

encountered were "savages"; slavery was just a way of life; and racism happened only in the South. Indigenous, Asian, Hispanic, African, and Muslim history rarely, if ever, made it into the textbooks.

Changes are happening, with more voices being added to the narrative to give a more rounded, balanced picture of U.S. history. Even today, though, if teachers are informed and have resources to share with students, they must be willing to do it. There are risks involved. For example, in 2021, an unarmed Black man named Jacob Blake was shot and killed by police responding to a domestic disturbance call. Two days later, a white teenager named Kyle Rittenhouse opened fire on a crowd, killing two people. Rittenhouse then walked up to armed police officers to surrender, wearing an assault rifle. But the officers ignored him, so he left the scene.

Teacher Matthew Hawn discussed the incidents with his high school students. He wanted to show them how systematic racism in the United States works. He explained white privilege, the unseen advantages that skin color gives some people over others. Parents complained, and Hawn was fired. Three days later, his home state of Tennessee passed legislation severely restricting how teachers can teach racism. Since January 2021, 44 states have taken similar steps. Lawmakers cited not wanting to make white children feel guilty and reducing overall feelings of patriotism. Lawsuits were filed in some states to fight the new laws.

Sometimes, a group or culture's history isn't taught—it's appropriated. Cultural appropriation is when parts of a culture, such as clothing, language, or music, are borrowed in ways that are disrespectful, stereotypical, or used for personal gain. It becomes even more apparent when white celebrities are praised for doing things that other cultures had already been doing for a long time. For example, Black students have reported being punished for wearing their hair naturally, in dreadlocks, or for wearing head coverings. But in 2015, celebrity Kylie Jenner wore her hair in dreads on the cover of *Teen Vogue*, and people praised her for it. In another example, the Japanese manga and anime *Ghost in the Shell* was so popular that Hollywood turned it into a live-action movie. But instead of casting an Asian actor in the lead role, filmmakers cast white actor Scarlett Johansson. Insiders reported that producers had tried to use technology to make the cast look more Asian.

Cultural appropriation is often rooted in colonialism. For years, Indigenous people were forced to give up their culture to integrate into white society. Practicing their way of life was illegal until the American Indian Religious Freedom Act passed in 1978. But now, selling Native culture has become popular. Consumers buy dream catchers, headdresses, jewelry, and smudge sticks without understanding their historic significance. The items themselves may or may not have been made by Indigenous hands, either. That means that the purchase price often doesn't find its way back into that community.

Abundant inequalities still exist in the United States. The U.S. Government Accountability Office compiles reports about race and shares them with Congress. They track subjects such as education, voting rights, equal employment, and health care. Their 2022 report found that there was a significant gap between what white people and minorities experience as they live their daily lives.

The COVID-19 pandemic radically changed the world in 2020. Nearly seven million people lost their lives. The virus showed Americans how unprepared they were for a global pandemic. It

Police in riot gear

ZOOM IN: TRIBAL GOVERNMENTS

The first American Indian reservation was set up in 1786. Reservations were areas of land set aside for Indigenous people. However, their main goal was to control the tribes and keep them apart from white settlers. Indigenous people were not considered U.S. citizens until 1924. Today, there are 537 independent tribal nations in the United States. Indigenous people live and govern on their own lands. The tribal governments take care of all the people on the reservation. They manage things such as garbage disposal, roads, and law enforcement. As of 2021, native groups have lost 99 percent of their original homelands.

An American Indian family living on an Oregon reservation in the late 1800s

also highlighted the disparity between racial groups. Black and brown Americans were much more likely to get COVID-19 and twice as likely to die from it. They were more likely to live in overcrowded communities, which increased their risk. They also had less access to health care, doctors, and healthy food. Their work environments were less flexible, too. The option of missing work or working remotely was rare.

Attacks against Asian people in the United States rose during the pandemic, as well. Thousands of incidents of anti-Asian discrimination were reported in the first year. Hate crimes increased by 169 percent. Verbal harassment, including racial slurs, being spit on, and physical violence were reported. One survey found that 1 in 3 Asian people feared they might be attacked. Small businesses with Asian owners lost money or closed. Language barriers made filling out paperwork for financial aid difficult. Government aid largely ignored minority-owned businesses at the beginning of the pandemic.

The media—and even the president—didn't help matters. After President Trump Tweeted about "the China virus," more than 700,000 Tweets containing 1.3 million anti-Asian hashtags were published. By attaching a location to the pandemic, it applied blame to an entire country and people, even though it wasn't their fault.

Believing Western medicine to be superior also slowed the country's response to stopping the spread of the disease. People in Southeast Asia have been wearing face masks to keep out both pollution and infection since the early 20th century. The practice began when an influenza pandemic led to the deaths of between 20 and 40 million people across the continent. Face masks never went away. U.S. health officials were skeptical about the effectiveness of masks and did not recommend them at first.

Protesters march and take a knee for a more just world.

CHAPTER 4:

The Road Ahead

Racism has been a part of the United States since the country was founded, and it is still woven tightly into today's society.

While activists fight for greater equality, others try to suppress them. Whether it's talked about or not, racism is a continuing problem. It can be easy to call it out but hard to change.

In 2021, a prom-posal in Minnesota made the news for its racist language. "If I was Black, I'd be picking cotton," the teen's sign said. "But I'm white, so I'm picking you." In 2022, a TikTok video went viral. Football players at a high school in California pretended to "sell" their Black teammates at a mock slave auction. In 2023, white girls at a Catholic school took video of themselves in blackface, mocking Black History Month. There is a long history of white entertainers painting their skin to look dark, depicting Black people in a negative light. The teens were expelled, but others have come forward with claims that the school has a history of not addressing racist incidents.

Social media has made incidents like these more visible. It can help minorities who feel isolated in white-dominated areas feel less alone. People who want to learn more about anti-racism can get helpful information online. Business owners and school

Black Lives
ALWAYS
matter
NO Peace
#BLM

administrators can find diversity consultants or other experts to help train employees on proper responses to new race-related situations.

However, social media can also make the problem worse. It is very easy to share a status, article, or meme without fact-checking it or thinking about it at all. Such posts can be shared hundreds, thousands, or even millions of times. They may be created by bots or spammers. There are also very few rules about what kind of content can be shared.

Some people hope a post-racial America will exist someday. In it, everyone, regardless of their race, would be equal. No one would have more opportunities than anyone else. There would be no discrimination, no prejudice, and no judgment. Some people believe the United States is there now. But research, facts, and first-person accounts prove that that belief is untrue. Race impacts the decisions people make. Conscious or unconscious biases can affect how they act on them. Having the privilege to ignore those facts does nothing to change the future.

Implicit racial bias is one obstacle in the way. These are biases and prejudices that are automatic and unintentional but still affect opinions and judgments. For example, many studies have shown that white people associate Black people with criminals—without being aware of it.

Another obstacle is denying a person's racial identity. Statements such as "I don't see color" and "All lives matter" are harmful. No matter how many times they are said, a person of color cannot change their race, their hair, or the way they look. They cannot change their life experiences. Those statements don't make them any safer in society. A person who makes those statements is denying their own implicit bias, too. They are denying that they could be thinking of, and treating, people of other races differently. Those phrases tell minorities that their

ZOOM IN: REPARATIONS

Hundreds of years of discrimination, enslavement, and exploitation gave white people a financial boost, resulting in a huge wealth gap between white families and people of other races. During slaveholding years, white people benefitted from free labor forced from Black people. Even after slavery ended, minorities were not allowed to own property, get a quality education, or hold high-paying jobs. They were essentially locked out by structural racism. The myth of "pulling yourself up by your bootstraps" ignores the fact that racism, discrimination, and Post Traumatic Slave Syndrome have made it impossible for minorities to control their destinies in the same way that a white person could.

experiences don't matter or aren't happening. It's a form of white privilege to ignore what Black and brown people experience every day.

Some of those experiences are generational. The last living person born to an enslaved parent died in 2022. Slavery was abolished just a few years after his father was born. His grandparents were enslaved in Virginia. The family told stories about their lives. The trauma of losing loved ones can last for many years. Generational trauma is passed from parent to child as Post Traumatic Slave Syndrome (PTSS). Physical and mental issues, stress behaviors, and even cultural mannerisms are part of this. And PTSS didn't end with slavery. Actions against the Black community into the 21st century continue to cause pain, trauma, and physical and emotional damage.

Groups such as Black Lives Matter, the National Association for the Advancement of Colored People (NAACP), the Southern Poverty Law Center, and the Native Justice Coalition are working for change. These groups defend the rights of people and promote their heritages. They understand that race is tied to the way people live in the United States—even though race has nothing to do with it.

In *Between the World and* Me, Ta-Nahesi Coates says, "All our phrasing—race relations, racial chasm, racial justice, racial profiling, white privilege, even white supremacy—serves to obscure that racism is a visceral experience." The emotions and feelings we find difficult to ignore are sometimes hard to struggle through. But they—like racism—shouldn't be ignored.

Getting Real

GEORGE FLOYD

George Floyd was a 45-year-old Black man living in Minneapolis, Minnesota. On May 25, 2020, a convenience store clerk called 911. He said Floyd had used a fake $20 bill. The police showed up shortly after and put Floyd in handcuffs. When Floyd refused to cooperate, white officer Derek Chauvin forced him to the ground and restrained him with a knee—even as Floyd said he couldn't breathe and lost consciousness.

The incident was caught on camera and circulated quickly online. Protests were held around the United States. It was the largest racial justice movement since the civil rights movement in the 1960s. The National Guard was sent to 28 different states. Dozens of cities enforced curfews. Police shot rubber bullets and tear gas into crowds. Marchers blocked freeways. Some protests were peaceful. Others involved looting or setting structures on fire. People were angry when no charges for the officers responsible for Floyd's death were immediately evident. "We tried doing it all peacefully," one protester said, "but they haven't heard us."

The officers involved were eventually charged, tried, and found guilty. The George Floyd Justice in Policing Act was introduced and passed through the House of Representatives in 2021. Its goal was to increase accountability for law enforcement and restrict the use of certain policing practices. But senators could not agree on terms, and the bill died on the Senate floor.

TA-NEHISI COATES

Ta-Nehisi Coates is an award-winning writer who explores race, politics, and society. His father was a Vietnam vet, member of the Black Panther party, and book publisher who specialized in books by Black writers. His mother was a teacher.

A Beautiful Struggle was his first published book. It followed his father's life and Coates' own childhood. His second book, *Between the World and Me*, won the National Book Award. It was a letter from Coates to his teenage son about what it means to be Black in America. A book of essays, *We Were Eight Years in Power*, reflects on the presidency of Barack Obama and its effect on the country's history. *The Water Dancer* is a work of fiction. The main character is an enslaved man in Virginia who is granted magical powers.

Coates also wrote the relaunch of Marvel Comics' Black Panther series. King T'Challa's kingdom, Wakanda, is a fictional country in Africa. Coates wrote a story during a time of upheaval, with citizens rising up against the royal family. T'Challa must work to find balance between the monarchy and the people.

Coates encourages readers to discuss the Black experience through Black eyes, rather than through the American Dream view. He describes the gap between those two experiences and highlights the fact that holding onto the Dreamer view ignores the Black struggle and the pain that was endured to get there.

Timeline

1607
The Jamestown Colony is founded.

August 1619
The *White Lion* sails into Fort Monroe, Virginia, carrying enslaved Africans.

1768
The first American Indian reservation is established.

1830
President Andrew Jackson signs the Indian Removal Act.

April 12, 1861
The Civil War begins.

January 1, 1863
President Abraham Lincoln issues the Emancipation Proclamation.

April 9, 1865
The Civil War ends.

July 9, 1868
The 14th Amendment is ratified into law.

1879
The Carlisle Indian Industrial School opens and operates for nearly 30 years.

1882
The Chinese Exclusion Act is signed. It is not repealed until 1942.

1932
The Tuskegee experiment begins. It lasts until 1972.

December 7, 1941
Japan attacks Hawaii, bringing the United States into World War II.

February 1942
Executive Order 9066 sends thousands of Japanese Americans to internment camps.

August 28, 1963
More than 200,000 people participate in the March on Washington for Jobs and Freedom in Washington, D.C.

June 12, 1967
The Supreme Court rules on *Loving v Virginia*, abolishing laws forbidding interracial marriage.

September 11, 2001
Al-Quada hijacks four planes, flying two into the World Trade Center in New York City.

January 7, 2020
Public health officials report a new form of coronavirus in China.

May 25, 2020
George Floyd is killed by police officers in Minneapolis, Minnesota.

Glossary

abolitionism—the promotion of ending or abolishing something, especially slavery

amendment—a formal change to a law or document such as the U.S. Constitution

colony—a territory under the control of another country and occupied by settlers from that country

discrimination—applying different treatment to someone based on factors other than individual merit, such as race, gender, or income

exclusion—being barred from entering or participating

Executive Order—a signed, lawful directive from the U.S. president that bypasses approval from Congress

immigrant—a person who comes to live permanently in a foreign country; a foreign-born resident

Indigenous—relating to the earliest known people in a place, especially a place later colonized

internment—the act of being confined, especially during wartime

militia—an armed group formed by private citizens

prejudice—an unfavorable opinion or judgment based on incomplete knowledge

rhetoric—artful speaking or writing that is often meaningless or insincere

segregation—being kept apart, usually based on race or class

stereotype—a widely held, fixed idea about something that is usually oversimplified or disrespectful

Selected Bibliography

American Civil Liberties Union. "Racial Profiling Since 9/11 Report." February 2004. https://www.aclu.org/report/racial-profiling-911-report.

Brown, Dee. *Bury My Heart at Wounded Knee.* New York: Rinehart & Winston, 1970.

Coates, Ta-Nehisi. *Between the World and Me.* New York: Spiegel & Grau, 2015.

DiAngelo, Robin. *White Fragility: Why It's So Hard for White People to Talk About Racism.* Boston: Beacon Press, 2018.

Jackson, Taryn. "Racism in America." PBS. January 24, 2022. https://www.pbs.org/articles/racism-in-america.

Kendi, Ibram X. *Stamped from the Beginning: The Definitive History of Racist Ideas in America.* New York: Nation Books, 2016.

Websites

Britannica Kids: Racism

https://kids.britannica.com/kids/article/racism/632495

Learn about the history of racism and its effects.

Time for Kids: Reflecting on Racism

https://www.timeforkids.com/g56/reflecting-on-racism

Find out what kids in the United States think about racism.

Index